Songs on the South Bank

Chris Ashley

Illustrated by
John Dillow

WALKER BOOKS
LONDON

For my parents

First published 1989 by Julia MacRae Books
This edition published 1992 by Walker Books Ltd
87 Vauxhall Walk, London SE11 5HJ

Text © 1989 Chris Ashley
Illustrations © 1989 John Dillow
Cover illustration © 1992 Shelagh McNicholas

Printed and bound in Great Britain by
Richard Clay Ltd, Bungay, Suffolk

British Library Cataloguing Publication Data
A catalogue record for this title is available
from the British Library.
ISBN 0-7445-2350-8

1

MY EYES HAVE SEEN THE GLORY OF
THE CUP AT MANOR PARK,
MY EYES HAVE SEEN THE GLORY OF
THE CUP AT MANOR PARK,
WE'LL GET IT BACK WITH ONE ATTACK
COULD DO IT IN THE DARK,
AND THE PARK GO MARCHING ON.

GLORY, GLORY MANOR PARK,
GLORY, GLORY MANOR PARK,
GLORY, GLORY MANOR PARK,
AND THE PARK GO MARCHING ON.

MANOR . . . . MANOR . . . .

Robert Naylor pulled the duvet closer in to his
neck and hunched his shoulders. He was trying to
eke out a few precious moments of warmth before

the dreaded rattle of tea cups, rap on the door, and Dad's gruff 'Up and at 'em', signalled the start of another school day.

The knock didn't come and Robert risked opening an eye to look at the bright green numbers flashing on his bedside clock-radio. "9.05! – Dad?"

Panic rising to his throat, Robert bucked out of the cocoon and was being strangled by a pyjama top before any real thinking took the place of his school day reflexes.

It was Saturday.

Robert's panic turned to a saint-like calm and he lowered himself back to a lying position with the same holy smile that Old Benfield, his headmaster, pulled when singing hymns in assembly.

Saturday.

A lounge around in his dressing gown watching the telly; a family party tonight; and before that, the 'Big One': First Division Manor Park United at home to Blackburn in the third round of the F.A. Cup. Brilliant!

The excitement that was still surging round his body from the early shock suddenly rose again to the surface. With a fist saluting the air Robert burst

the silence with a mighty – "United!" – and ignoring the bangs on the wall from his parents' room he congaed his way along the landing and down the stairs:
"Manor's going to Wembley,
Manor's going to Wembley,
La la la la, la la la la!"

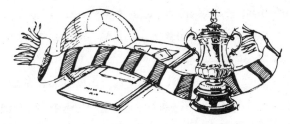

If Robert Naylor thought he was going to spend his Saturday morning lounging around in pyjamas he had another thought coming – at least that was what a businesslike Mrs Naylor informed him. "I've got a houseful tonight, Rob, and I need all the help I can get."

The party was for Nan, whose seventieth birthday it was, and Robert had looked forward to it all week. He loved family parties; aunties saying how tall he was getting and then looking shocked when they saw what was in his glass: "Do you really have a shandy now, Robert?" Uncles would ask about his football and tonight they'd all listen as he talked Grandad through the Big Game.

The whole family were Manor Park supporters but Grandad especially. He wasn't allowed to go any more but he still knew the players, and Robert took great pride in telling him every detail and making his reports as good as possible. "Old Grandad won't even listen to the score till you've spoken to him," Nan had once told Robert.

He'd forgotten about those terrible hours before the party, though, when the house had to have a major tidying-up job done on it; and now that he was approaching thirteen, Robert supposed he was expected to do more than sort out a few records and keep out of the way. Oh well, a bit of work now would make the afternoon seem even better. He pulled himself up from the settee and purposefully switched off the cartoon that his sister Stacey had been watching.

"Mum!"

Robert pulled a face and made his way out to get dressed. Bad news, though, was on its way downstairs with Dad.

"Come on Rob, throw your clothes on. It's you and me on the old shopping trolley today, son."

Robert groaned.

"We're going over to the new superstore by the tunnel to get the party food and picking up Nan and Grandad on the way back."

Now Robert couldn't believe his ears. "Dad! It takes nearly half an hour to get to the tunnel, and Nan and Grandad live right over by the Manor Ground. We'll never do it all before the match!"

Then came Dad's bombshell. "It's the party, Robert. Football's out for you and me today. Sorry, son."

"But Dad!" This was unbelievable. "Dad, we've got to go!" Robert was chasing him up the hall to the kitchen. "Dad!"

Mr Naylor turned. He wasn't budging. "Sorry, Robert. I've got too much to do and there's no way you're going to that football ground without me; they're mindless animals some of those lads. It's bad enough when I'm with you."

Robert was going to cry at the unfairness of it all. He hadn't missed a home match all season and now he had to miss the F.A. Cup! He felt his lip begin to go...

No! Crying was the last thing that would get him to the match. He would have to play this as a grown up: so he struggled to fight the tears, his mind racing while he waited for his voice to come under control.

Then he had it. Devon Dougan!

"Devon! What about Devon, Dad? I could go with him and Mr Dougan." Devon Dougan lived in the next street and was Robert's closest friend at school. The Dougans never missed a game and followed much the same Saturday match routine as Robert and his dad. They even parked up the same road and always stood with the Naylors in Manor Park's special family enclosure.

Mr Naylor was caught off-guard. He liked Devon and his father. Mr Dougan would take good care of Robert, there was no doubt about that. But Robert could hear the doubt in his dad's voice.

"Oh, I don't know, Robert. You know what it's like for them – all of those idiots in the crowd making those...well...You know, noises and silly comments."

Robert knew exactly what his dad meant and was

just as embarrassed. The Dougans were a West
Indian family and the colour of their skin made
them an easy target for just the sort of mindless
followers of football that Mr Naylor was worried
about. There was a silence while Dad filled the
kettle and Robert struggled to find something to
say.

"Oh come on, Dad... The Dougans wouldn't go
to any matches if they let that sort of thing bother
them." He wasn't at all sure, though. He'd seen
Mr Dougan's strong grip tighten on his son's arm
when the noises had started: and he'd seen the
surprised hurt in Devon's eyes as all around him
supporters of his own team, Manor Park, East
Londoners like himself, had changed into a baying
mob just because a black player from another side
had got the ball. The sheer ignorance of it always
shocked Robert, too. Manor Park had three black
players in their own first team, and one of them,
Les Small, was Manor's only England
International. What did the baying idiots think
happened to Small's skin, or his feelings, when he
pulled on the red shirt of Manor Park?

But Robert didn't let his disgust stop him

pressing home his claim. He had to go. "Come on, Dad. I'm nearly thirteen and Mr Dougan will look after me."

Mr Naylor was obviously wavering. He had begun vigorously rubbing his unshaved cheeks, a sure sign that he was thinking hard. Robert's eyes pleaded. Dad stopped rubbing and his hand slammed down onto the kitchen counter. "Oh, go on then, Robert. Go round to Devon's house and ask Mr Dougan very nicely if he'll take you."

"Yeah? Oh, well done, Dad!"

The decision was made, but Mr Naylor wasn't happy; he was worried. Robert being at the football without him made him feel somehow out of control of things; and when Mr Naylor lost control, his temper usually went too.

"I don't know. I just don't know. You kids! I always take you to football and you won't even miss one match to help your mum and me out."

He swore and began clanging the tea pot. Robert made a quick move upstairs to get washed. He understood his dad's worries and if it were just any match he might have given up. But this was the F.A. Cup!

From upstairs ten-year-old Stacey had been watching developments closely and now she began her revenge for the switched-off TV. She tip-toed along to the bathroom door and then hammered on it loudly.

"Come out, Robert. I need to get washed so I can help Mum and Dad."

Robert cringed, she'd chosen the best possible form of attack.

"Come on, you've been in there hours, you great pansy!"

That really got to Robert. He exploded out of the bathroom and along the corridor, while from the safety of her swiftly shutable doorway Stacey rocked her stomach in laughter. Robert lunged at the gap, missing by a long way.

"Dad! Tell Robert."

Mr Naylor assumed that the fuss was still about

Robert being in the bathroom and he added his annoyed weight to the argument. "Robert!" he shouted. "Stop being so soft – you haven't got time to make yourself pretty. There's work to be done. You can go the Co-op on your way to Devon's for a start. Mum needs flour quickly for her sausage rolls."

A scarlet Robert threw on his clothes and began going down when Stacey sing-songed her final attack. "Softie, softie...making himself pretty."

That was it! Robert crashed down the rest of the stairs. "Nobody calls me soft!" he screamed and pulled open the front door – crashing it shut with such force that his stomach somersaulted as he waited to see if the frosted glass was going to break.

2

WE'RE ON THE MARCH WITH MANOR'S ARMY,
WE'RE ALL GOING TO WEMBLEY.
AND WE'LL REALLY SHAKE 'EM UP,
WHEN WE WIN THE F.A. CUP,
'COS MANOR PARK'S THE GREATEST
FOOTBALL TEAM.

Robert sprinted down his street, heading, he
supposed, for the shops. All the time he was sure
that he could feel the eyes of Dad, who must have

come to the door, boring into his back. "Nobody calls me soft," he mouthed again to himself, trying to keep his anger going. He rounded the corner onto the small shopping parade which was crawling rather than bustling with those too old, too young or too poor to be part of the superstore generation. Noisily he pushed his way into the tiny Co-op.

"Flour, flour, sausage rolls."

Robert's eyes skimmed the shelves, and, eventually finding three powdery bags, he made his way to the check-out, just pushing ahead of two pensioners who tut-tutted at the rudeness of the younger generation. The manager who had already exchanged a sympathetic look with the elderly ladies, two regulars, rang up the two pounds ninety and sat drumming his fingers; a busy man.

Then it hit Robert. He hadn't picked up any money when he stormed out. He made a big show of tapping his pockets, but he knew there was nothing there. What a morning!

"I haven't got any cash," he croaked.

"Well, what have you got then? American Express?" The manager lifted his bushy eyebrows to make sure the two ladies were in on his joke.

They were only too pleased to be involved and looked at each other and then at Robert as if this was God punishing him for pushing in.

"I haven't got anything," he said.

"Oh great, well that puts my till out. Thanks a lot!"

Robert stared at the floor.

"Well, go on then. Put it back. I don't know. These youngsters, in such a rush they don't care how much work they create for others..." The manager was changing the till roll now and talking to the whole queue while the pensioners waited for a loud, "Excuse me" before moving aside to let Robert back to the bakery shelf...

The flour returned, Robert stumbled out into the weak winter sun, with a face the colour of the Manor Park jerseys.

A loud snigger made him spin round before he could even get his breath. "What a show up, Naylor!"

Robert couldn't believe this. It was Damien Blake from school. He was in for a rough ride now!

Good-looking and oozing easy confidence, Damien Blake wasn't the type to take the micky now, though. Oh no, he'd wait until there were a few more people around to enjoy it, like at school on Monday. But his twinkling eyes let Robert know that he hadn't heard the last of this little incident.

"What are you doing here, then?" Damien asked with a chatty smile.

"Nothing much," replied Robert, staring him out.

"Going to the Blackburn game this afternoon?" Damien was still grinning.

"Yeah, course I am."

The two of them moved slowly off, Damien booting an empty cola can into the road with a great clatter.

"We'll give 'em a good thumping this afternoon, eh Rob?"

"Yeah." Robert's smile was half-hearted. Did Blake mean the Blackburn team or the supporters? It was hard to tell: Damien was always talking about the fights he'd seen at matches. Anyway, Robert decided not to show himself up again by asking.

"Going with your dad are you, Rob?" The

laughing eyes again. Everything he said made Blake sound like the world's friendliest kid – but Robert knew him. Behind the smiles, Damien was making fun. You wouldn't catch me with my dad in the family enclosure, the wide grin seemed to be saying.

But for the first time since early that morning Robert cheered up. He made a big show of making up his mind: "No, I won't bother with my old man today..." he eventually replied, as if sniffing the air to decide how best to spend his afternoon. "I'll probably go down with Devon – old Dougan." That was one in the eye for Blakey, he wouldn't have been expecting that!

Surprisingly, though, Damien's grin only got wider. He stopped walking and looked straight into Robert. "Oh, come with me instead then, Rob; on the South Bank. Join 'The Firm'."

Silence! The eyes weren't laughing now. Robert should have known. All the talking, all the friendly smiles; it had all been leading up to this. The challenge.

The Firm was the name given to the Manor Park supporters who stood under the South Bank stand

and made most of the noise during home games. They prided themselves on causing problems at all matches, and usually ended up in the papers after rioting on away trips. No one would dream of standing with them unless they wanted trouble. Supporters from Robert's age group often went up there just to be part of it, to watch and sometimes even be involved in the violence that was always part of the day.

Robert shook his head. Join The Firm? What a joke! Blake knew there was no chance of him, Robert Naylor, going onto the South Bank: but he'd had to ask. Oh yes! Blake wanted to hear him back out, to hear him avoid trouble like he did at school. Blake wanted to be able to call him soft on Monday when he told everyone about the show-up in the Co-op.

Robert lifted his eyes slightly and looked at Damien who'd started whistling now, waiting for the backdown. Game, set and match – Damien Blake. Well, Robert Naylor would show him! He'd show everyone! He finished examining a crack in the pavement and allowed himself to meet Damien's cold blue eyes. Soft. So that's what they all thought, was it? Well, Rob Naylor wouldn't be backing down. He wouldn't be wheeling around a supermarket trolley this afternoon and he wouldn't be in the family enclosure.

He'd be on the South Bank cheering his team on. Why not? He knew the songs. He knew the form.

Just somebody try and stop me, he said to himself. Tears were only just behind his eyes and his nails had dug into his palms. He hated Blake for this.

But Robert brought himself under control, he wanted to say it right... He took a breath and, yes, he could trust his voice. "Yeah, O.K. then, Blake. I might as well go with you. What time?"

Robert regretted it almost as soon as it came out. The South Bank was a dangerous place. Dad would have a heart attack if he found out – and it was going to involve Devon in a lie. Damien had been genuinely surprised. His eyes had widened for a split second. "Yeah?..." he'd said, stunned. "Er, right, you're on then, Rob...Welcome to The Firm." He ruffled Robert's hair and the cocky grin came back while his brain must have been working overtime, finding a last dig to try to get the upper hand again. And he managed it. As both boys turned for home he called out: "Oh, Robert..."

Robert looked back, frowning. He just wanted time to think.

"Don't wear the bobble hat Mummy knitted, will you?"

"I haven't got a bobble hat," Robert growled: and despite the doubts, the guilt and the fear that were already crowding his mind, Robert knew that if he ever wanted to face anybody in school again, there could be no turning back now. He had to go with Damien, he had to stand on the South Bank and join The Firm.

3

WE ARE MANOR, WE ARE MANOR,
SUPER MANOR
FROM THE PARK.
WE ARE MANOR, SUPER MANOR,
WE ARE MANOR FROM THE PARK.

Every icy particle of January air carried the fever of
a big match that afternoon. Robert had been
infected since his first sighting of the 102 bus with

MANOR GROVE, FOR MANOR PARK UTD written on the front.

At the ground, taking a risky jump from the still moving bus and following the others towards the stadium, his senses were bombarded by the occasion. His eyes were filled with red and white until the grey metal curve of the East stand reached above the scarves and the clouds of tobacco and hot-dog smoke into the pink London sky. Hamburgers and onions tempted his nostrils as now one cheek and now the other was warmed by each food stall that he passed. But it was his ears that told him this was really a big one. From inside, above the excited chatter, the bellows of programme sellers, hot-dog vendors and the roasted-peanut man, Robert could hear the tantalising snippets of a large crowd enjoying the pre-match entertainment.

The Dagenham Girl Pipers, or some such band, must have been fighting a losing battle against the early arrivals on the South Bank. The Firm, as always, seemed to have their own Manor Park song or rude words to every tune that was banged out on the xylophones and whistled through the loudspeakers.

The rest of the crowd were loving it, judging by the laughter and applause, and as Robert strained to hear more there was a huge jeering cheer; either some unfortunate marcher had dropped a baton or the Blackburn supporters at the other end had tried to join in the fun and not done very well. Robert almost hugged himself. It was all part of the excitement – what an afternoon at football was all about. No television cameras could bring this into a front room. Feeling a great wave of warmth and affection for his game, his club and his crowd, Robert turned to line up for a programme.

A good-natured hand yanked him away. "You don't need one of those on the South Bank, Rob."

It was Damien. Robert laughed and followed him as he jauntily picked his way through jostling supporters and puffing police horses. He only just stopped himself from putting out a hand to grab Damien's arm, the way he held Dad's when they needed to stick together in a big crowd. Robert allowed himself a quick smile at his near mistake. He could afford it; the afternoon had gone well so far.

By the time he'd got back from his run-in at the Co-op, Dad had already left for the superstore and Mum had been too busy to do more than tell him to be careful and to do whatever Mr Dougan said. Obviously the slammed door incident was to be forgotten and Stacey's sulking face confirmed that she'd had a good telling off for her part in the affair. Mum had even been too harassed to notice that he'd put on his best jeans and Pringle jumper for the match. The bobble hat comment had hurt.

Just as he'd shouted his goodbye and tried to sneak out without his clothes being spotted, the phone had rung and Robert's conscience had forced him to answer it.

"It's Grandad, Mum. Wants to know if there's any last-minute bits he can get for the party."

"Well, you'd better tell him we need sausage

rolls, after your little stunt with the flour this morning."

"Sausage rolls, Grandad."

"O.K, son. Tell your mum I'll shoot out to my freezer man on the High Street and pick some up."

But Mum had been worried. Robert's grandparents lived right near to the Manor Park ground. "Tell him I don't want him out and about in that football crowd."

"Mum says . . ."

"I heard," Grandad had interrupted. "You tell your mum that if Adolf Hitler's army couldn't stop me in 1944, I'm not going to be worried by a few football fans."

Typical Grandad.

The phone call over, Robert had got away and made for the bus stop. He'd gone the long way round in case Stacey was nosing from the window and wondered why he hadn't gone down Devon's street; a good touch, he thought, and he'd done well on the bus, too. All of the lads from school were on it and Robert had known Damien would be out to show him up, if he could. But the hour or so he'd had since they'd parted outside the shops had given him time to plan a reply to Damien's obvious challenge to have a cigarette. "No thanks, I don't want breath like yours," he'd said. That got a laugh from a couple of the girls with them on the top deck and Robert had grown in confidence. But something else was helping too. Damien's attitude seemed to have changed. Instead of goading Robert into looking a fool, he now seemed to have taken on the role of protector, as if he was proud of having recruited a new member for The Firm and saw it as his job to look after him.

Yes, things were going far better than he'd expected: but now, rounding the corner from Manor Grove, Robert's heart missed a beat as he saw the entrances to the South Bank for the first time on a match day.

The biggest difference from his normal entrance was the number of policemen on duty; and he couldn't quite believe it as one of them searched him. Searched him, Robert Naylor, in the queue to get in! He didn't know whether he should try and look hard or try and show the policeman, through some secret signal, that he wasn't really a hooligan and only came round here to be with his friends. He must have ended up pulling a really stupid face because Damien laughed out loud and said, "They'll be cracking up in the van at that mug you were pulling." Robert didn't know what Damien was on about until he followed his pointing finger and saw a police video camera trained on the next boy being searched. "That puts you in The Firm now."

Dean Fosgate, another kid from their class confirmed, "They'll have your face up at the Yard by now. Britain's number one wanted man – Robert Naylor."

Dean and Damien found this hilarious, but Robert could only think of dawn police raids on his house after The Firm's next away-game rampage and his feeling of well-being disappeared.

4

WE'RE ON OUR WAY TO WEMBLEY,
WE SHALL NOT BE MOVED.
MANOR'S GOING TO WEMBLEY,
WE SHALL NOT BE MOVED.
WE ARE THE TEAM THAT'S GOING,
TO WIN THE F.A. CUP,
WE SHALL NOT BE MOVED.

A still worried Robert paid his money, showed his identity card and climbed his way up the dark steps ready for his first taste of life in The Firm. He didn't know if the churning in his stomach was fear, excitement or an eagerness to get out into the open and become part of the mountainous noise that was coming from the top of the stairs; it was almost deafening. He stopped to listen.

"United. . . United," and then claps that sounded like machine gun fire as they bounced off the tin roof and bare concrete walls. Robert couldn't stop a grin coming to his face and Damien obviously felt infected, too.

"United," Blakey shouted, still on the steps, but Robert was too shy to join in. . . yet. Finally at the top and into the crisp air, he allowed himself a few seconds to drink in the scene: the bright green pitch under the early afternoon floodlights; some players in blue tracksuits (obviously Blackburn) warming up at the other end; and over to one side the family enclosure where he would normally be standing with his dad.

He stood on tiptoe and thought he could just make out Devon and Mr Dougan reading the programme, but didn't get time to look any closer. A great clamour from behind told him that the rest of his bus load of fans had got in and were anxious to get out into the open, too. Another great cry of "United", a sharp push in the back and Robert found himself being sent clattering down the tiny terrace steps and bang into a 'Rambo' combat jacket. He cringed, real physical fear turning his legs to jelly.

The wearer of the jacket stopped waving a fist at the Blackburn end and turned, murder written in his look. Robert's heart sank further as he saw the spiked black hair and the ear stud; he knew this bloke! He was in the fifth year at school, a real hard case and definitely someone to avoid. A pair of thin lips parted in an animal snarl and blazing eyes bored into Robert. . . but then lifted to the entrance where the rest of Robert's school contingent were still piling through the gap. A look of confusion and then recognition crossed the murderous face – and incredibly changed it into an indulgent grin.

"All right, my old son?" he said, steadying Robert's arm and then pointing to the Blackburn end. "Save your attacks for that lot, eh?"

The relief that surged through Robert's body was one of the strongest feelings he'd ever known. It wasn't just that he'd escaped a beating up; there

was another feeling that this boy's friendliness –
and the whole afternoon so far – had given him. He
realised what it was and for a split second of clear
understanding knew what had saved him just now,
and what made people gather under stands like this
all over the country. They must all feel like he did
at this moment. . . He belonged.

No two life-styles could be more different than
his and the one he guessed that his new 'friend' led,
but today they both belonged to the same
something. The school? The Firm? Manor Park?
London? Whatever it was, it wouldn't last long
(Robert would steer well clear on Monday). But for
now, with the incredible noise of all the others who
belonged ringing in his ears, it was enough –
"United!" came the roar again and Robert joined in
the claps as, breathing again, he grinned his way
back to Damien and the others.

"United!" Yes, United. United meant together,
didn't it? And that was what they all were,
thousands of them. United. Together. And it was
great.

The next ten minutes were brilliant. The ground
filled to bursting point and The Firm turned their

attention from the marching band to the Blackburn supporters. They went through their repertoire of songs with such volume that Robert wondered if his ears could take it. It was so loud that he felt no embarrassment at joining in now, and as he and Damien jigged up and down to the Manor Park version of 'Hark the Herald Angels', Robert wondered why he didn't always come up here. What was so bad and dangerous about it?

"Hark now hear the Manor sing,
Blackburn run away,
The Firm will fight forever more,
Just watch us go today."

At last, Robert spotted people beginning to applaud in the stand opposite the tunnel and he knew that the players were coming. He hadn't thought anything could be noisier than the singing, but when The Firm caught its first glimpse of red shirts coming chewing, waving and stretching towards them, Robert felt the strange sensation of screaming as loud as he ever could, yet still not hearing his own voice at all.

5

WHEN PARK GO UP
TO GET THE F.A. CUP,
WE'LL BE THERE,
WE'LL BE THERE.
WHEN PARK GO UP
TO GET THE F.A. CUP,
WE'LL BE THERE,
WE WILL BE THERE.

The South Bank went through the names of the
Manor Park players in turn and gave an extra loud
cheer to individual favourites like the captain, Steve

Sharp, who responded with a short, embarrassed wave. Robert's giddy feeling of enjoyment died for a few moments when he thought of how his dad would have been loving this moment. They'd have been checking the programme together now and eagerly awaiting the opposition to see who was playing for them. Blackburn had a few big names worth watching.

Feeling something like homesickness for his normal place on the family terrace, Robert again stretched on his toes to try and pick out the Dougans: and again it was a mistake. He lost his footing, not stumbling down steps this time, but being carried in a human wave as a scuffle or something caused the packed crowd to move.

But a strong arm was holding his. It was Damien, unruffled and still smiling. "Steady on, Rob. We don't want to lose one of The Firm!"

Forgetting the family enclosure, Robert felt a fierce stab of pride and affection. He couldn't see what he'd ever had against Damien: he was a good mate.

"Here they come!" shouted Damien, and whatever else he said was lost as the South

Bank, Robert included, booed the first two Blackburn players out of the tunnel. It was great; even Robert managed to work up a feeling of hatred towards the visitors. It was as if he owed it to The Firm; and as he gulped in the breath for a fresh boo he found himself almost tipsy, giggling out loud like a kid on a roundabout.

Damien, again strangely knowing, put a proud arm around Robert and they began the next boo together, laughing hysterically. Then suddenly, the noise changed and Robert felt the hatred around him grow far stronger. The faces under the old tin roof were twisted now and making different noises. He strained above the backs of the people in front for a view of the players' tunnel to see what had happened; and he realised immediately. Looking awesome, with muscles bulging under his oiled black skin and crisp blue and white shirt, Trevor Walker, Blackburn's fearsome striker, was jogging his way up to the visitors' end, receiving a rapturous waving of blue and white scarves there, and a chorus of hatred from the rest of Manor Park.

Robert looked away and started trying to

convince himself that it was Walker's goal scoring ability that made him the enemy of this crowd. But he knew it wasn't. And as the screaming continued, he glanced at Damien, an arm still proudly round his shoulder, and saw that his face was contorted and heard his voice screeching above the others. Damien's grip tightened and Robert began to boo again; the same boo he'd given all the Blackburn players, not the one the rest of the South Bank were giving this gifted player. Damien's grip grew stronger still and Robert, with tears in his eyes, continued booing. He knew that to everyone around it looked as if he was making the same noise as them. Did he want it to look that way? He tried not to answer that, but he couldn't stop his thoughts going to where, about fifty metres away, somebody else would be feeling a strong grip on his arm. Instead of shame that person would be feeling great hurt.

Robert closed his eyes. "Sorry Devon," he mouthed.

6

WHEN MANOR PARK,
GO MARCHING IN,
OH WHEN THE PARK GO MARCHING IN,
I WANT TO BE IN THAT NUMBER,
WHEN THE PARK GO MARCHING IN...

The atmosphere around Manor Park crackled, and even The Firm grew quiet as the great minute hand on the clock above the West stand shuddered towards three. Robert got himself as comfortable as he could in the crush and for the first time really thought about the match.

A win today and he would have a radio under the science bench on Monday, ready to hear the fourth round draw. Tottenham or Arsenal at home would be nice. But almost as soon as Manor Park kicked off to a fantastic chorus of "Come on, you Reds! Come on, you Reds!" it became obvious that the fourth round was a long way off. Blackburn were not top of the Second Division for nothing.

As usual at this time of year, Manor Park's entertaining, skilful brand of football was getting bogged down on a muddy surface. They were trying too hard. Blackburn's more direct approach, with long accurate balls aimed at the head of Walker, was having far more effect and only four superb saves from Knight in the Manor Park goal saved the First Division side from embarrassment in the opening quarter of an hour.

The South Bank remained quiet during this early period of Blackburn domination and Robert was surprised at the intelligent football talk that went on around him. Damien had scorned a programme but he and lots of others seemed to know the Blackburn players, and surprisingly gave them credit for some of their good moves. Of course, nobody went as far as to applaud them.

After twenty minutes the inevitable goal came. Deep in his own half, Steve Sharp tried to be too clever and lost the ball. The Blackburn player who had beaten him found himself with time to tee up a perfect cross which Walker nodded past the flapping Knight with ease.

In the other parts of the ground the goal was greeted with a stunned silence. But on the South Bank chaos broke out. There was an obvious attempt to get on to the pitch and over at the dancing mass of blue and white at the Blackburn end. Robert was expecting it but again he lost his footing as hundreds of larger bodies hurtled down the terraces. He didn't know how he avoided going under, but almost at pitch level the avalanche stopped and allowed him to gulp in great lungfuls of cold air.

The angry South Bank settled back to its old position like a stormy sea being sucked out ready to crash in again. Thankfully, though, it settled, but uneasy and ready for another surge at the slightest annoyance.

There were shouts for the handful of Firm members who had got on to the pitch and who were now being led away by the Police; but from then on the cheers were few and far between. There was no fun in the air any more. The mood was ugly. A few taunts of "You only sing when you're winning!" broke out from isolated groups around him, but there were no more of the mass choruses which had raised such an incredible noise and been so fantastic to be involved in earlier.

Most people were just staring; looking not at the pitch and Manor Park's desperate efforts to get back into the game, but either straight at the Blackburn end or towards each other, exchanging grim smiles and meaningful nods.

Robert found it unpleasant and strange at first, but he made the most of the calm to get into the game. Being a goal down to a Second Division club was part of the F.A. Cup magic, and he could see this game building into a real cracker. Blackburn were strong at the back and looked quite capable of breaking away again to go two up. Half-time was approaching, but the men in red just kept running in to the hard Blackburn tackles. They were holding on to the ball for too long. He shook his head, annoyed. Davey Pierce on the wing was the worst offender and, as he lost the ball again, Robert complained out loud, "Pierce is rubbish, he won't learn will he?"

There was no reply. Robert turned to Damien and Dean and found himself looking at their backs. They were fiercely scanning the crowd behind.

"I said, Pierce is rubbish!"

Damien half-turned. "You what, mate?"

"Pierce," Robert repeated above the angry shouts from other critics around the ground, "Rubbish!"

But already Damien had turned back. Robert gave up. Neither Damien nor Dean were taking the slightest notice of anything but the faces in The Firm above them.

The half-time whistle brought an end to the frustration and was greeted with a chorus of boos. Robert took the opportunity to rest his aching neck and waited for the baiting of the majorettes band who were twirling their way nervously over the mud towards them. But the South Bank weren't interested this time. All eyes were focussed on the same area of the terrace that Damien and Dean were staring at. What was up there? All Robert could see was a small bald man in a huge overcoat. Why was he so interesting? And why did he get a whole metre of clear space around him while all the rest of The Firm were squashed together like sardines?

"What's up with old Baldy then?" Robert asked Damien.

"Shut up, you idiot! Shut up!" Damien was obviously petrified and shot frightened looks around. So Robert did shut up. His first ever sight of a frightened Damien Blake had done it. He'd had enough.

7

WELL, WEMBLEY'S IN OUR HISTORY,
AND IT'S ENOUGH TO MAKE YOUR HEART GO
OH, OH, OH, OH, OH!
WE DON'T CARE WHAT THE OTHER TEAMS SAY,
WHAT THE HECK DO WE CARE?
THE ONLY THING WE KNOW IS
THERE'S GOING TO BE A SHOW,
AND THE MANOR PARK BOYS WILL BE THERE.

"Right! We go!" Damien nudged Robert, who
swung round puzzled.

He'd been staring at the match. There were

about fifteen minutes left and Manor Park were still a goal down and getting nowhere. He didn't really care. He was cold and the mood here frightened him; really frightened him. In fact, he realised, he'd only been looking at the game to avoid meeting any of the dangerous eyes that surrounded him, and now: "We go!" What did that mean? Go where? The whole of the South Bank seemed to be on the move, though, disappearing through the exits looking like bathwater swirling away. He followed Damien, feeling pressure from behind. They were right in the middle of the mass departure. "What's going on?" Robert shouted as soon as they reached the hold-up at their exit and had to stand still while those in front descended into the darkness.

"I'll tell you on the way round," Damien shouted back.

"Round where?"

"Round to have Blackburn, of course! That's what we're here for, isn't it?"

Robert's ears buzzed and he felt winded. Damien was right. Of course fighting was what they were here for. And if it wasn't dangerous then it wouldn't have been such a big dare to come. That was why everybody had accepted him, why he'd belonged. They'd all assumed that when this moment came, when the fighting started, he'd be there.

The fighting. Robert let the words go round in his head. Fighting. There was going to be a fight and he, Robert Naylor, had to be in it – or at least near it. He looked back at the floodlit pitch and then at the family enclosure. He would do anything, give anything to be there right now. Why had he been so stupid?

The exit cleared and it was Robert's turn to go down. He'd had no chance to turn, to stay on the terraces or to do anything but move with this great mass of bodies heading for trouble.

Suddenly they were out. Two things hit Robert – first, it was incredibly cold now he wasn't crunched up in the huge crowd; and secondly, it was dark. There were no floodlights out here and night had closed in. Everyone was walking, not running or singing, heading for the corner of Manor Grove.

He was tempted just to make a break for it here. But what would this lot do to him if he tried that? Perhaps he could pretend to tie up his laces or something? But there were more and more of them coming out behind him all the time; and anyway, at that moment, Damien put a pally (or was it a secure?) arm around him and started to explain.

"Loads of the Blackburn lads will be leaving early to get on their coaches and keep out of trouble. Well, we've got a few of our lads up at their end; they give a signal when the Blackburn lot are beginning to go."

Robert made no reply.

"Old Baldy as you called him is the Boss. You know, Boss? Firm? Get it? He's hard, Rob, very hard. You don't call him anything – you stay away! Anyhow, he waits for the signal and decides when we go round. Then, zap!!"

If Damien had hoped for some enthusiastic

response, he was to be disappointed. They had reached the corner of Manor Grove now and Robert was feeling freezing cold and boiling hot all at the same time. Apart from the splashing sound of their marching trainers, The Firm weren't making any sound at all and above the noises from inside the stadium he could hear his own heart pumping with a sort of hissing sound. There was just the length of the West Bank stand to go now before it all started. Just one football pitch to go before...

Robert didn't dare to even think about what was going to happen.

8

MR VENABLES SAID TO GEORGE GRAHAM,
"HAVE YOU HEARD OF THE LADS
AT TOTTENHAM?"
GEORGE SAID, "NO, I DON'T THINK SO,
BUT I'VE HEARD OF THE MANOR, AGGRO!"

The mob had stopped and Robert, blindly
following, had stopped, too. His insides jumped.
There up ahead was the best sight he'd ever seen:

grim-faced, with drizzle shining on silver badges, was a line of policemen. The Firm couldn't get round! There wouldn't be a fight! But Robert's relief didn't last for long.

"High Street!" came a voice from the front.

It was like a war, Robert thought; the generals had it all planned.

The mob turned for the High Street which ran alongside the ground, separated only by a long parade of shops. They could get round that way. The need for secrecy had gone and they were walking quickly now, arms high in the air chanting and clapping. As they rounded the corner to the High Street, they broke into a trot, daring anyone to get in the way.

The boys in Robert's group, camp followers, had fallen in at the back and were trailing a few metres behind the older mob. The constant chanting – "Manor, clap, clap, clap," – brought back memories of before the match when it had all seemed fun. But there was no fun now – at least, not Robert's kind. This was a nightmare unleashed on the waking world; Robert's world. Mothers were crouching, desperately holding children inside the

shop doorways of the busy High Street; people
were running to cross the road and cars had
stopped, their drivers unwilling to crawl past an
army on the march...

And Robert was part of it.

Things were getting nasty now. Caught up in the
thrill of the advance, some had started kicking over
dustbins and shop displays. But shopkeepers stayed
inside, preferring to lose a bit of stock than face the
savages outside. Excitement mounted, the chanting
got louder and they were running; it was a rampage.

Robert ran with them – frightened of being left
alone and blamed when the mob had gone. Up
ahead he could hear glass breaking. The army had
found a bus shelter and were demolishing it.
Petrified shoppers were just standing as carrier bags
were flung up into the night, groceries raining
down into the gutter. This seemed like fun to

Robert's group. There was no danger; nobody was doing anything to stop it; so they started booting around the bags that had landed near them and throwing the spilled shopping at the bus stop opposite.

"Here you are, Rob! Chuck one!" And Robert found a bag of sugar pushed into his hand. He was almost in a trance now and didn't know what to do. He dropped the missile at his feet, waiting for the chorus of disapproval from Damien and Dean. But they weren't interested. Up ahead, attention had turned from the bus stop to the people sheltering in the large, well-lit entrance to 'Arctic Fresh', the huge freezer store which dominated that stretch of pavement.

"Here, you leave that alone, you young ruffian!"

There was a huge cheer. Resistance at last. After it had been threatened all day, this section of The Firm prepared to see real violence for the first time.

There wasn't actually much to see. Just a scattering of people from the doorway and Dean hurrying the boys at the back along.

"Come on! Someone's getting done!"

Robert followed, not just scared of being alone this time but because something had disturbed him. Something really bad, worse than what he'd seen and been involved in so far. He ran with the others. What was it?

"Put that down, I say."

Now Robert knew. He recognised that voice. He loved that voice. Who else would be brave enough, stupid enough, to stand up to these animals?

"Grandad!"

It was a shout, but Robert didn't know if any sound came out, he just kept running towards the voice. Several things, silly things, were to stick in his mind afterwards: the face of the boy running next to him who was so excited that he had to do little dances as he ran, and the stickers on the 'Arctic Fresh' window advertising the chance to win a new Fiesta car. But what Robert knew he'd never never forget was the sight in the shop doorway. Sitting down where he'd fallen, head in his hands, was Grandad. He was sitting as a frog sits: bottom on the floor and knees up around his head. His razor-creased trousers had ridden right up his thin shins leaving a pair of brown checked socks on display which somehow seemed indecent, something you shouldn't be looking at. The shoes still had their army shine which reflected the light from the shop window, but the rest of the soldier's pride in Grandad had been spilled onto the patterned tiles with his glasses, his hat and the sausage rolls. That was what hit Robert; not the blood on Grandad's forehead and on his nose where his glasses had been, but that loss of dignity while the brave old soldier sat rocking his head slowly and showing his brown checked socks.

As the stunned Robert watched, a kindly woman went to the old man and began to try and lift him. Grandad just sat still, his head still moving from side to side as he reached for his hat and brought his old shopping bag into the safety of his lap where he could guard it even more closely.

"Go! Go! Go! – Police!" The shout had come from the mob. The damage done, they were already dispersing; but now The Firm stampeded, leaving Robert staring open-mouthed at the horrible scene in the doorway.

Grandad finally seemed to take on a form of life and looked with puzzlement at the woman trying to help him. He lifted his head to look where the attack had come from. For a second his eyes seemed to settle on the paralysed Robert; but since Grandad's glasses lay broken beside him, Robert couldn't tell whether the old man knew him or not.

The lights were closer now and a siren could be heard. But Robert was stuck to the spot, he couldn't move. He was the only one left and as he heard a car door slam he knew that he really should be moving; either getting away or helping Grandad. But his legs wouldn't go. A rough hand grabbed him from behind and Robert prepared to turn to the Police Officer. He didn't care now.

It wasn't a policeman. It was Damien, he'd come

back for him. "Come on, move! You'll get done for this!" And Damien pulled him along, Robert stumbling as he looked back to the giant freezer shop, seeing nothing but the reflections in a pair of shining shoes sticking out onto the pavement.

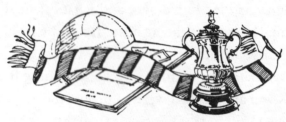

The leaders had always had bigger fish to fry and they were still making for the Blackburn end of the ground. The road where, ages ago, Robert had jumped from his bus was filling up as the crowd began its departure, and now the kids at the back of The Firm again began their look-out for the pickings left behind by the leaders.

Not Robert though. For the first time that day he managed to get himself going in the opposite direction of The Firm members. And he ran, ignoring the From Damien, from Dean and the other ran. He ran, not really knowing the other heading, until his lungs couldn't gasp in any more oxygen and until the ringing of "United! United!" had died in his ears. Then he leaned against a car and waited.

It wasn't until Devon and Mr Dougan came along chatting excitedly that he realised what road his frenzy had led him down, and what car he'd somehow known to lean against. He said nothing on the drive home, not even when Mr Dougan pulled over to let an ambulance go screaming by; and Devon and his dad were somehow too sensitive to try to break into his thoughts.

back for him. "Come on, move! You'll get done for this!" And Damien pulled him along, Robert stumbling as he looked back to the giant freezer shop, seeing nothing but the reflections in a pair of shining shoes sticking out onto the pavement.

The leaders had always had bigger fish to fry and they were still making for the Blackburn end of the ground. The road where, ages ago, Robert had jumped from his bus was filling up as the crowd began its departure, and now the kids at the back of The Firm again began their look-out for the pickings left behind by the leaders.

Not Robert though. For the first time that day he managed to get himself moving in the opposite direction of The Firm members. And he ran, ignoring the shouts from Damien, from Dean and the others; he just ran. He ran, not really knowing where he was heading, until his lungs couldn't gasp

in any more oxygen and until the ringing of
"United! United!" had died in his ears. Then he
leaned against a car and waited.

It wasn't until Devon and Mr Dougan came
along chatting excitedly that he realised what road
his frenzy had led him down, and what car he'd
somehow known to lean against. He said nothing
on the drive home, not even when Mr Dougan
pulled over to let an ambulance go screaming by;
and Devon and his dad were somehow too
sensitive to try to break into his thoughts.

9

WE'RE THE BARMY,
MANOR ARMY,
LA LA LA LA LA LA.
WE'RE THE BARMY,
MANOR ARMY,
LA LA LA LA LA LA!

The family were all sitting round together. They
weren't in the Naylors' front room, though, eating
party food and listening to Robert's match report.

They were gathered round a bed in the Royal Docks Hospital.

Grandad had needed some stitches but although badly shaken he wasn't seriously hurt. All the same, old Uncle Jack's joke, "What are we all looking so happy about?" had stunned everybody into silence.

"We're taking Nan to have a word with the Sister, Uncle Jack. You and Robert look after Dad."

"What?"

Uncle Jack shook his hearing aid and Mrs Naylor, eyes to the heavens, turned to Robert. "You stay with Grandad and make sure old Jack doesn't wander off anywhere. Honestly, I should have left him with next door instead of Stacey..."

Robert, who hadn't said anything since getting in from the match, just nodded. Everybody else had been too involved with the family emergency to pay him any attention. The adults moved off and Robert looked at his grandfather's grey face, a huge plaster covering his forehead and the stitch on his nose looking spikey and strange.

Grandad's eyes opened and he looked at Old

Jack munching a bedside banana, and then he looked at Robert. He took his grandson's arm and shook it.

Did Grandad know he'd been there? Robert focussed his thoughts for the first time. But it was an affectionate hold, and Grandad attempted a smile.

"Enjoy your game, son?"

Robert started to say something, but nothing came, only tears. Grandad knew. A young hand found an old one and Robert sobbed openly and unashamedly. Jack had found an orange now and wasn't interested. Grandad let the boy sob and then started talking again. His voice was faint but Robert could hear him. He was telling a story or something.

"You know, when I was a boy, there was this character round our way called Mickey Finnigan. He was a bit older than us but we all wanted to be in with him. Well, once me and a couple of others hopped school to spend the day with him."

Robert looked up. What was this all about?

"Well, we had a dip in the river and on the way back we found this great plank of wood, a bit like a telegraph pole, and we all carried it back to Finnigan's street. I thought that was it and I was just about to go home, when Finnigan called me back and dared me to help him lean the pole against some old boy's door, knock and then run. You know, a bit like 'Knock down Ginger'..."

Robert sniffed and nodded, puzzled. He'd stopped crying now and was listening carefully.

"Well, the difference, of course," said Grandad, his voice growing stronger, "was that when the door was opened this great pole would fall in on the old boy's head..."

Robert was all ears now. "Did you do it, Grandad?"

"Yes, I did it. I wanted to stay in with Finnigan. But thank the Lord the old chap came round the back to see who was knocking and never opened the front door. But my word he was lucky!" Grandad paused, looking at Robert and then pulled a handkerchief from his pyjama jacket which he dabbed at Robert's eyes and his running nose. "I've been ashamed of that day for about sixty years now, and I've had to live with it. But I learned my lesson. I stayed away from Finnigan, I knew what he was like. I stuck to my old friends, proper friends, played my football. I even got a trial for Manor Park once, you know."

Robert was crying again now; old Grandad knew him.

"Come on, cheer up, son. I'm all right and what about my old team, eh? An equalizer with five minutes to go, the nurse said. We'll beat them in the re-play. Blackburn have had their chance."

Robert looked up. All that and he hadn't even known the score.

"Who do you fancy in the next round?" Grandad asked. "Liverpool? Tottenham? I expect you'll be going down with that mate of yours. What's his name – Devon?"

Robert smiled. "Yes," he said. "I'll be going down with Devon."

Grandad winked, gave a soldier's salute and laid himself down on the pillow. "I need some sleep now, son." He opened his eyes again and shook Robert's arm one more time. "Oh, and Robert... Take old Jack away before he eats all my fruit."

Robert laughed. "Come on, Uncle Jack," he said. The two of them walked down the ward,

Robert's thoughts racing, but one picture in his mind: him, Devon, and the two dads together in the enclosure for the fourth round. He smiled and in his mind he began to sing:

"Manor's going to Wembley, Manor's going to Wembley, La la la la...la la la la."